Best Barks!!!

♡ Manya + JZ

Jack Chaps

JACK CHAPS, DOG DETECTIVE:

The Curious Case of the Cow & the Great Chicago Fire of 1871

Pen•sive Paws Publishing Co.

Jack Chaps

For my Mother, editress extraordinaire, my Father, and family.
For the many, many friends and individuals who have helped or encouraged . . . .

A portion of the proceeds from this book will be donated to no-kill animal shelters in Chicago.

www.JackChaps.com

Jack Chaps, Dog Detective: The Curious Case of the Cow
& the Great Chicago Fire of 1871 © 2015 by Marya Lucas

Text by Marya Lucas
Photographs and Drawings by Marya Lucas

Graphic Design by DeAnna Clark and Photo Editing by Caitlyn Eakins
Graphic Consultation and File Preparation by Alex Osterman
Business Consultant, Robert RPC Gibbs

Printed in the USA by Worzalla in Stevens Point, Wisconsin.

Published by Pen•sive Paws Publishing Co.
Library of Congress Cataloging-in-Publication Data is available (2014906164).
ISBN: 978-0-9960629-0-9

One **BRIGHT** summer morning in Chicago, Jack Chaps, dog detective extraordinaire, **SNIFFED** something in the air.

"*Biggs Quigley!*" said Jack Chaps to his favorite Fat Cat.
"My ears are particularly WIGGLY...
and my nose detects a MYSTERY."

Biggs pawed through the paper, *PAWpular Times*,
and listened to the little dog rhyme . . .
And, that is when he saw it.
The bold letters of the news headline **POPPED** out,
and Biggs gave out a **SHOUT!**

"LEGEND OF THE COW AND THE GREAT CHICAGO FIRE LIVES ON!!!!!"

"JACK CHAPS!" exclaimed Biggs.
"Little dog, large ears, you have a
nose with a **KNACK.** There is indeed a
mystery — a mystery of a **FIRE IN A
HAYSTACK.**"

PAWPULAR TIMES

From the newspaper, Biggs read: "The story goes . . .
Long ago, one dark night when they were all in bed,
Old Mrs. O'Leary lit a lantern in her shed,
Daisy **THE COW KICKED IT OVER,** winked her eye and said,
'There'll be a hot time in the **OLD TOWN** tonight.' "

"And, boy," said Biggs, "was that cow right!"

"The flames from the lantern engulfed the shed. Then, across the city of Chicago they spread, rising hotter and higher, until . . . **KAPOOF** . . . Chicago was on **FIRE!**"

OCT. 11, 1871.

JACK CHAPS and BIGGS stared at each other with EYES open WIDE!

The LEGEND OF MRS. O'LEARY'S COW must be *cast aside*.

With a look of DOGGED DETERMINATION on his face, JACK CHAPS said:

"Biggs, I shall race to **CRACK THIS CASE!**
I feel it in my bones, I know not how,
BUT THAT FIRE WAS NOT CAUSED BY DAISY THE COW!"

So, with a rallying bark, Jack Chaps ran to Lincoln Park.
There, he found **FARMER LOU**, and his cow with a clue, Mr. Bovine.

BARK
ARF
BARK

greencity
MARKET

South End of Lincoln Park

"Why, if it isn't Jack Chappy, the **DOG DETECTIVE PAPPY!**" said Mr. Bovine.
"I'll tell you a clue. **DAISY WAS LAZY!** That milk cow would not start a fire.
Why, she'd rather munch grass all day than kick a lantern in the hay."

"BUT IF DAISY DIDN'T DO IT, THEN WHO OR WHAT DID?" ASKED JACK CHAPS.

"That's the mystery exactly, my friend,"
said Mr. Bovine, as he scratched his rear end.
"There is only one way to find out.
You must follow the route of the wisest cow yet,
MOO-STER BUMPY — *Master, Teacher, Swami, and Sensei*
of all things Chicago . . . of the CHICAGO WAY!
Surely he will know the history of this great mystery."

Moo-ster Bumpy

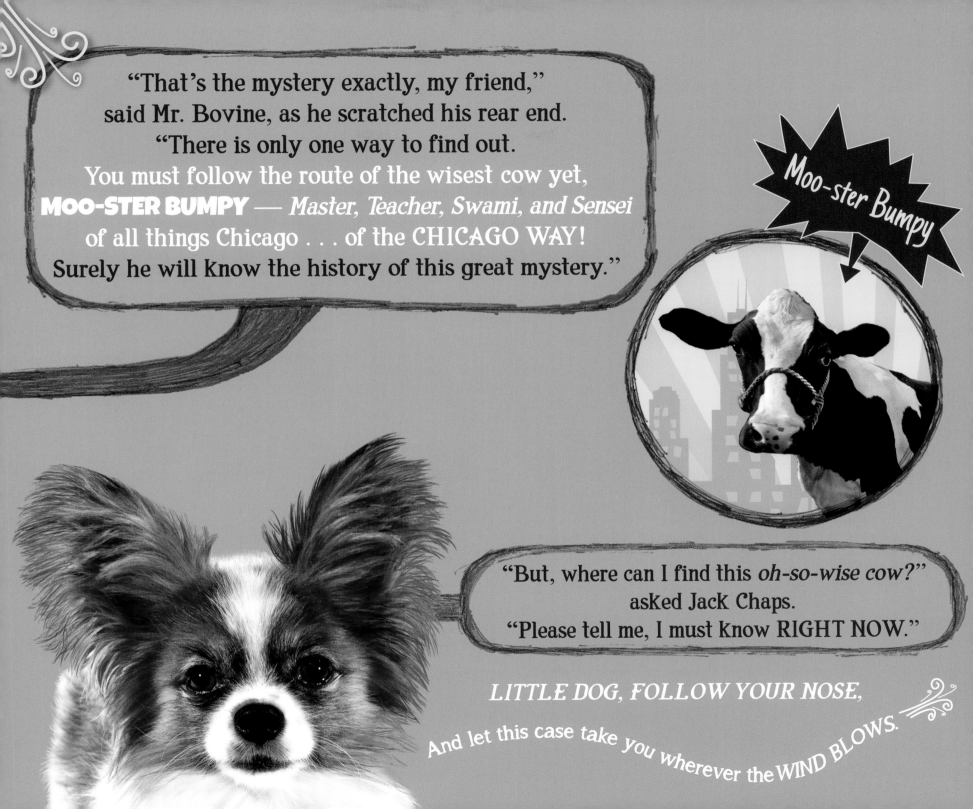

"But, where can I find this *oh-so-wise cow?*"
asked Jack Chaps.
"Please tell me, I must know RIGHT NOW."

LITTLE DOG, FOLLOW YOUR NOSE,

And let this case take you wherever the WIND BLOWS.

SO, WITH A SNIFF OF THE SUMMER WIND, JACK CHAPS CAUGHT THE SCENT OF COW.

HE BIPPED AND HE BOPPED TO THE ♡ OF DOWNTOWN, TO THE CRISS-CROSSED BUILDING THAT RISES SO HIGH, IT ALMOST SCRAPES CHICAGO'S SENSATIONAL SKY!

Biggs thought *Jack Chaps* might find that cow at the top of the **JOHN HANCOCK**. But that idea was a whole lotta **POPPYCOCK**.

Still, Jack Chaps **RUSHED** to the **94TH FLOOR**. He could see Lake Michigan, the cityscape, and more, but just as he suspected, there was not a cow to be detected. So, Jack Chaps turned around and **BIPPED** down to the ground.

"Fine Feathered Lady with your horse and carriage," said *Jack Chaps* with a **FLOURISH** and a **BOW,**
"Kindly tell me, have you seen a cow?"

"Why, yes, Jack Chaps!" she cried.
"Moo-ster Bumpy just took a ride!
To my delight, **HE MOO-ED** and
AAHH-ED at all the city sights."

"Great Scott, which way did that cow go?"
asked Jack Chaps.

"I think he's headed for a show!" said
Fine Feathered Lady.

JACK CHAPS
DASHED to the Theatre in
WATER TOWER WATER WORKS.
Moo-ster Bumpy, sadly, was nowhere to be found.

But that did not stop this
LARGE-EARED HOUND.
JACK CHAPPY, the dog detective PAPPY,
was on a mission to find that cow.

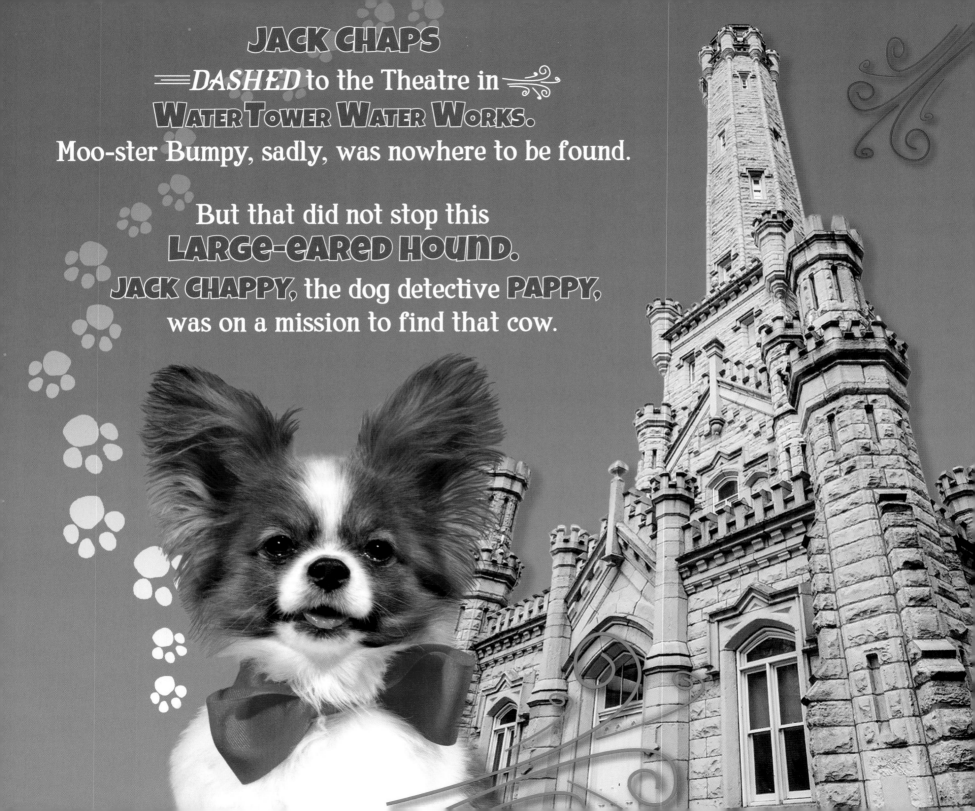

Jack Chaps **BIPPED** and he **BOPPED** to
FIRE STATION 98. But, Jack Chaps was just **TOO LATE.**
Moo-ster Bumpy had *come* and *GONE.*

"FANTASTIC FIREMEN, which way did that cow go?"
asked Jack Chaps, as the Firemen slid down the pole.
But, the Fantastic Firemen did not know.

★ ★ TO ★ ★

N Michigan Av

A Magnificent Mile

of **FANCY** shops,
Jack Chaps
BIPPED &
he BOPPED.

He saw the glitter, he saw the glitz, the BIG brown bags, and the ritz.

But he did not see one bit of Moo-ster Bumpy.

JACK CHAPS TROLLEY

"JACK CHAPS! DON'T GIVE UP NOW, FOLLOW THAT COW!"

said the Little Trolley Girl as her hair FLITTED and FLUTTERED . . . in the BREEZE.

"I JUST SAW HIM HEADING TO NAVY PIER!"

Jack Chaps ran as fast as his paws would go. He **HOPPED** and he **BOPPED** right onto the giant **FERRIS WHEEL.** He spun **HIGH,** he spun **LOW,** around and around he did **GO.** He was **RAZZLED** and **DAZZLED** by the wondrous city sights. But he did not see **MOO-STER BUMPY** even from that height.

NAVY PIER

DOCK STREET

Popcorn

Carousel

Funny Mirrors

NEVERTHELESS, JACK CHAPS COULD SMELL HIM IN THE AIR, SO HE KNEW THAT COW WAS NEAR. But he could not find Moo-ster Bumpy anywhere on the pier.

"Ah-ha, the ships, of course!" he yipped.
"*Ahoy Sailor Joe!*" cried Jack Chaps.
"Where must I go? I'm looking for a cow,
and I must find him right now."

"For goodness' sake, Jack Chaps, hurry, make haste!
I just saw Moo-ster Bumpy rounding that corner by the Lake!
He's headed to The Field Museum, no doubt,
so run along *Little Scout*."

"Right-O, Sailor Joe, off I goooo . . . !" said Jack Chaps.

But, he was already racing lickety-split along the Lakefront Path, passing BIKERS, RUNNERS, WALKERS, he was going so *FAST*.

The Field Museum was filled with marvels and more, collections of stuffed animals, artifacts, fossils, and plants galore, and best of all, SUE, the fierce ancient dinosaur!

"SUE!" *barked Jack Chaps excitedly,* "have you seen Moo-ster Bumpy, the cow that holds the key to the Great Chicago Fire Mystery?"

ROAR
ROAR
ROAR
ROAR ROAR

But, Jack Chaps, gumshoe extraordinaire,
quickly saw that SUE, the great *T. rex* dinosaur,
quite simply could ROAR NO MORE.

She had died long, long ago, and that's a fact.
Sixty-seven million years to be exact.

JUST THEN JACK CHAPS SAW HIS REFLECTION IN THE BEAN. LARGER EARS HAD NEVER BEEN seen!

AND, THAT IS WHEN IT HAPPENED. THE LITTLE DOG GOT DISTRACTED. HE FORGOT ALL ABOUT FINDING moo-STER BUMPY AND SOLVING THE FIRE MYSTERY.

His Large Ears Caught the Melodious Notes Carried by the Breeze from the Concert in the Park.

He STOPPED TO SMeLL THe FLOWERS OF THe LurIe GARDeN WALK.

He frolicked in the Fountain of Faces under the warm summer sun.

Jack Chaps was just having so much FUN!

"I LOVE Millennium Park . . . I will stay here forever!"

"But, Jack Chaps," said the Children, "IF YOU STAY AND Play,
You'll NEVER FIND MOO-STER BUMPY TODAY!
He's the cow that holds the KEY to the Great Chicago Fire MYSTERY!
Remember, you are a dog detective, a city sleuth,
and that's simply the DOGGONE TRUTH!"

Jack Chaps' ears **WIGGLED** to and fro.
He caught a *whiff* of cow, and he knew — *he knew* he had to go.
He **HOPPED** and he **BOPPED** right onto the **"L."**

"Jack Chaps, don't give up now," yelled the Conductor, **"FOLLOW THAT SMELL!** Go north to **LITTLE INDIA,** my friend — the last neighborhood before the city limits end!"

In a FLURRY, Jack Chaps SCURRIED.
But once there, all he could smell was the CURRY.
Amidst the spices and saris in this little neighborhood town,
Moo-ster Bumpy was nowhere to be found.

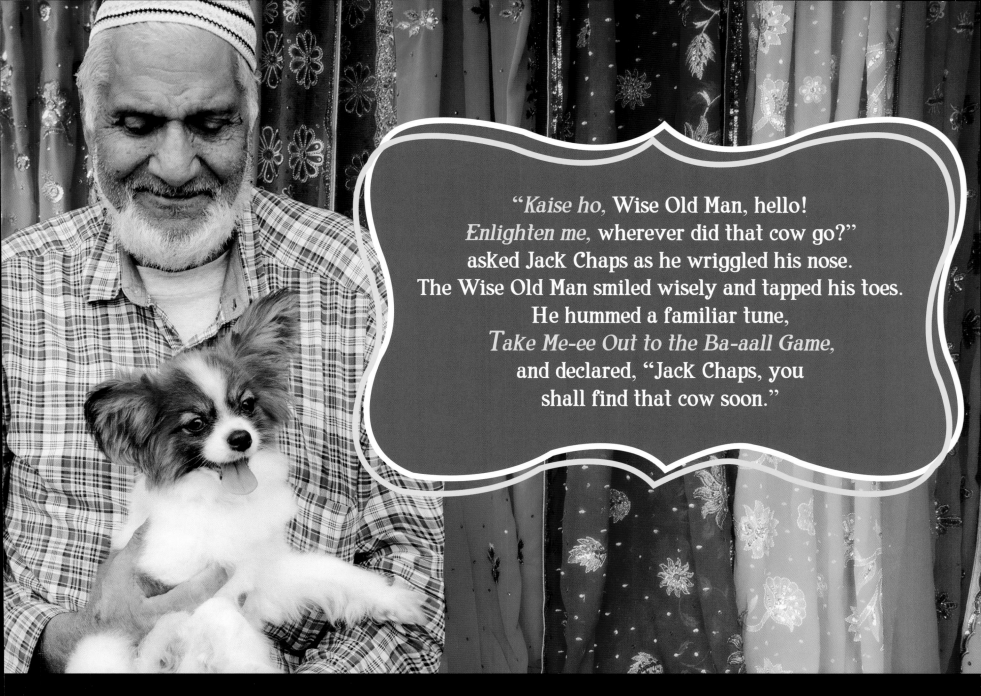

"*Kaise ho*, Wise Old Man, hello!
Enlighten me, wherever did that cow go?"
asked Jack Chaps as he wriggled his nose.
The Wise Old Man smiled wisely and tapped his toes.
He hummed a familiar tune,
Take Me-ee Out to the Ba-aall Game,
and declared, "Jack Chaps, you
shall find that cow soon."

Jack Chaps let out a **YIP**, and he let out a **SHOUT**.

"Of course, **BASEBALL!** Off I go to **WRIGLEY FIELD**," he cried out.

WRIGLEY FIELD HOME OF CHICAGO CUBS

JACK CHAPS!

DASHING into the park,
Jack Chaps stopped with a start . . . .

"HO-LLLL-YYY
COWWW!"

JACK CHAPS heard the sports announcer BARK.

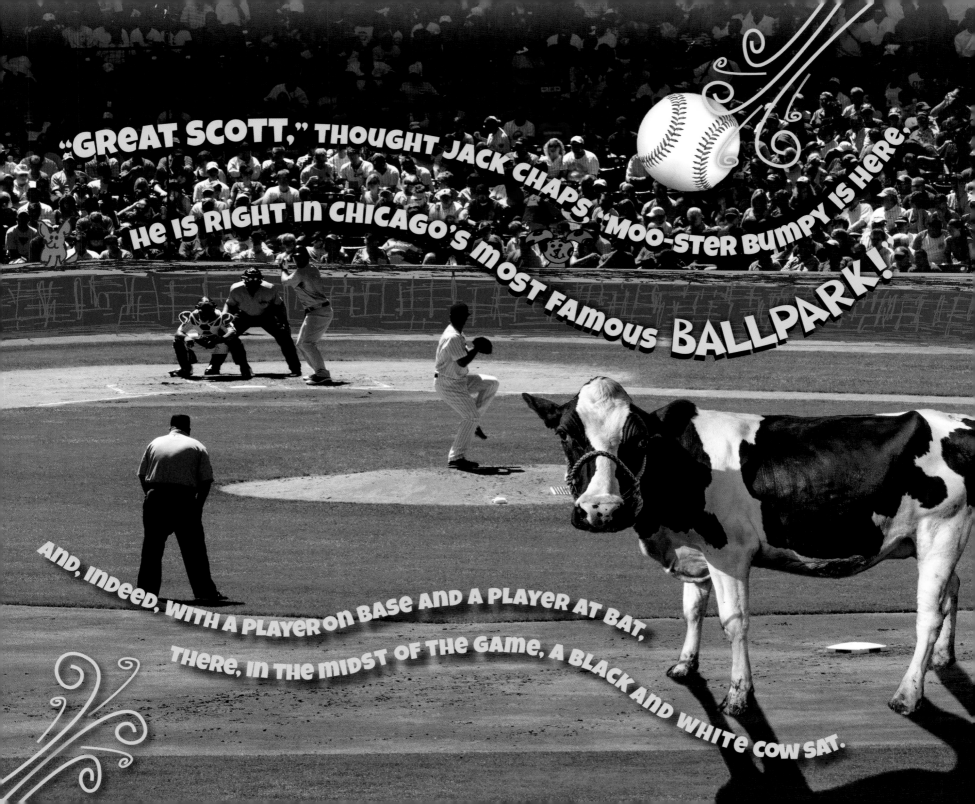

Onto that field Jack Chaps ran with all his might.

His *Butterfly* ears *Flitted* and *Fluttered*

Faster and Faster . . . until the little dog took **FLIGHT**.

Jack Chaps sailed upon the gentle *Breeze*

until he bumped *SMACK-DAB* into the wise cow's Knees.

Before Moo-ster Bumpy could utter a sound,
the **WIND** began to **WHIRL** all around.
Then, with a Zen-like sigh,
Moo-ster Bumpy winked one large bovine eye . . .

"Jack Chaps, the answer you seek
is *Swirling* at your feet.
It's *Fluttering* your ears and *Fluffing* your *Fur*.
It's closer than you think."

Jack Chaps knew that cow was giving him a **CLUE!**
What could it be, Mrs. O'Leary's **SHOE?**

And then, with a GUST of inspiration, the answer came to him.

It was not a COW or a SHOE . . .

It was the *WIND* that *BLEW!*

"THE WIND!" he barked, with a flourish and a bow.
"THE WIND toppled that lantern. That, I know now!"

"CHICAGO, the *WINDY CITY!*" EXCLAIMED THE EXCITED CROWD.

"MYSTERY SOLVED! CASE CLOSED!" SHOUTED *JACK CHAPS*,
AS HE CLAPPED HIS PAWS, AND THE CROWD ROARED ITS APPLAUSE.

And, that is how Jack Chaps cleared Daisy the Cow of blame. The history of the Great Chicago Fire will never be the same!

CHICAGO
CITY OF BIG SHOULDERS, CITY OF BIG EARS!

History: The Great Chicago Fire of 1871

While this story is fiction, Jack Chaps in reality is a very cute papillon with large butterfly ears (papillon = butterfly in French!). And, the Great Chicago Fire really did happen. This book highlights the mystery surrounding the cause of that historic fire, which erupted on Sunday evening, October 8, and raged until October 10, 1871.

The fire broke out in the barn of Patrick and Catherine O'Leary, located at 137 DeKoven Street on Chicago's West Side. But, no one knows exactly how. Within hours, however, rumors had spread as fast as the fire that Mrs. O'Leary and her cow were to blame. The first newspaper to print the story was the *Chicago Evening Journal*, which, on October 9, 1871, reported that, "The fire broke out on the corner of DeKoven and Twelfth streets, at about 9 o'clock on Sunday evening, being caused by a cow kicking over a lamp in a stable in which a woman was milking." Nonetheless, it is unclear how the newspaper obtained this information or how the rumor of Mrs. O'Leary and her cow came about. Mrs. O'Leary claimed innocence, reporting that she was in bed when the fire started. Newspapers at the time, however, were known for fictionalizing and sensationalizing stories. Also at that time, Chicagoans apparently wanted someone to blame for the destruction of their city. Because there were strong sentiments against Irish immigrants, like the O'Learys, they were easy targets.

From November to December 1871, Chicago authorities conducted an official investigation regarding the fire and heard sworn testimony from 50 witnesses, including Mrs. O'Leary. Yet, authorities concluded the cause of the fire was unknown. The official report stated: "Whether it originated from a spark blown from a chimney on that windy night, or was set on fire by human agency, we are unable to determine." This report, however, failed to salvage the O'Leary family's reputation, and the legend persisted.

Modern historians have discredited the O'Leary legend and have proposed other theories. Some historians, for example, believe that the O'Leary's neighbor, Daniel "Peg Leg" Sullivan (named for his wooden leg), started the fire; others believe that a spark from someone smoking lit the blaze; some suspect that boys, while shooting dice in the barn, knocked over a lantern; and, yet, others, that the fire was caused by a comet. Although justice took awhile, in October 1997 the Chicago City Council officially exonerated Mrs. O'Leary and her cow of all blame for starting the fire.

The Jack Chaps children's book proposes a relatively faultless cause of the fire: the wind. This explanation dovetails with reports of strong winds the evening of the Great Fire and also plays on Chicago's nickname as the "Windy City," which has a history in its own right. This story further encourages children, with the help of adults, to engage in historical questioning and analysis.

While the cause of the fire will never be fully known, we do know Chicago was unmistakably transformed afterwards. Although the fire destroyed approximately three square miles of the city, including buildings and businesses, and left many people homeless, Chicago resolved to rise from the ruins. The city recovered with incredible speed; according to one report, a man sought to collect bricks, still warm from the fire, for rebuilding. Above a shanty was scrawled: "All gone but wife, children and energy." With this can-do attitude, Chicagoans rebuilt a bigger and bolder city with modern architecture and skyscrapers. Fine examples include William Le Baron Jenney's Home Insurance Building and Daniel Burnham & John Root's Rookery and Monadnock buildings. The city flourished, and Chicago was once again an important midwestern center for culture, trade, and transportation. In 1893, only 22 years after the fire, Chicago hosted the World's Columbian Exposition. This World's Fair celebrated the four-hundredth anniversary of Christopher Columbus' discovery of America and attracted over 25 million people to the various cultural exhibits. It was proof that Chicago was the comeback kid among cities.

We hope you visit the new and rebuilt Second City of today, with its fascinating history, magnificent city skyline, beautiful Lake Michigan, kind-hearted people, and abundant culture.

A list of sources may be requested at JackChaps@gmail.com

My walls survived the Great Fire of 1871!

- St. Mike's in Old Town -

Special thanks to all entities that permitted the use of images in the book, including but not limited to:

The "Jack Chaps portrait" (pg 4, "Library Scene") is artwork by Krista Brooks of Retro Pets (RetroPets.com) and is entitled, "San Canine de Papillon - Patron Saint of Butterflies" | Wall artwork (pg 5, "Library Scene") is by my grandfather, Lloyd White, a cartoonist | Green City Market (www.greencitymarket.org) | Special thanks to dairy farmer Albert Lenkaitis (www.lenkaitisholsteins.com) and all other book models | Navy Pier (www.navypier.com) | Images used with permission of The Field Museum, Chicago | Cloud Gate© image used with the permission of artist Anish Kapoor | "Crown Fountain" image used with the permission of artist Jaume Plensa and © 2014 Artists Rights Society (ARS), New York / VEGAP, Madrid | Courtesy of the Chicago Transit Authority; only small, well-behaved pets in protective carriers or service animals are allowed on CTA buses and trains | Major League Baseball trademarks and copyrights are used with permission of Major League Baseball Properties, Inc.

CHICAGO MAP
(See Other Side)

Jack Chaps

THE JACK CHAPS MAP
CHICAGO, IL

1. **North Avenue Beach** Jack Chaps Begins his History Mystery Tour!

2. **Green City Market in Lincoln Park** Clark & Menomonee

3. **John Hancock Center** Don't forget to visit the 94th floor! Michigan Ave & Delaware

4. **Horse & Carriage Rides** Huron & Michigan Ave; Chicago & Michigan Ave

5. **The Chicago Water Tower (psst ... this building survived the Great Fire!)** Also, catch a show at the Lookingglass Theatre! Chicago & Michigan Ave

6. **Chicago Fire Department (CFD) Engine Co 98** Near Chicago & Michigan Ave

7. **Michigan Ave, the Magnificent Mile!**

8. **Chicago Trolley & Double Decker Co** Hop on by the John Hancock Center

9. **Navy Pier** Ferris wheel, sailing, & more! Grand Ave, east of Lake Shore Dr

10. **Lakefront Trail** Bike, run, or walk along this 18-mile path!

11. **The Field Museum with dinosaurs and more! Museum Campus** Roosevelt Rd, east of Lake Shore Dr

12. **Millennium Park with Jay Pritzker Pavilion, Cloud Gate (aka the Bean), Crown Fountain, and Lurie Garden** Between Randolph & Monroe, just east of Michigan Ave

13. **Chicago Transit Authority (CTA)** Red Line "L" Stop at Monroe & State

14. **Devon Avenue, spices and saris!** Western & Devon Ave

15. **Wrigley Field, Chicago Cubs** Addison & Clark (Also, catch a **Chicago White Sox** game at US Cellular Field, 35th & Wentworth!)

16. **The Chicago Theatre** State & Lake The Jack Chaps History Mystery Tour Ends, and the Jacksonian Era Begins!

¡GO CHICAGO!